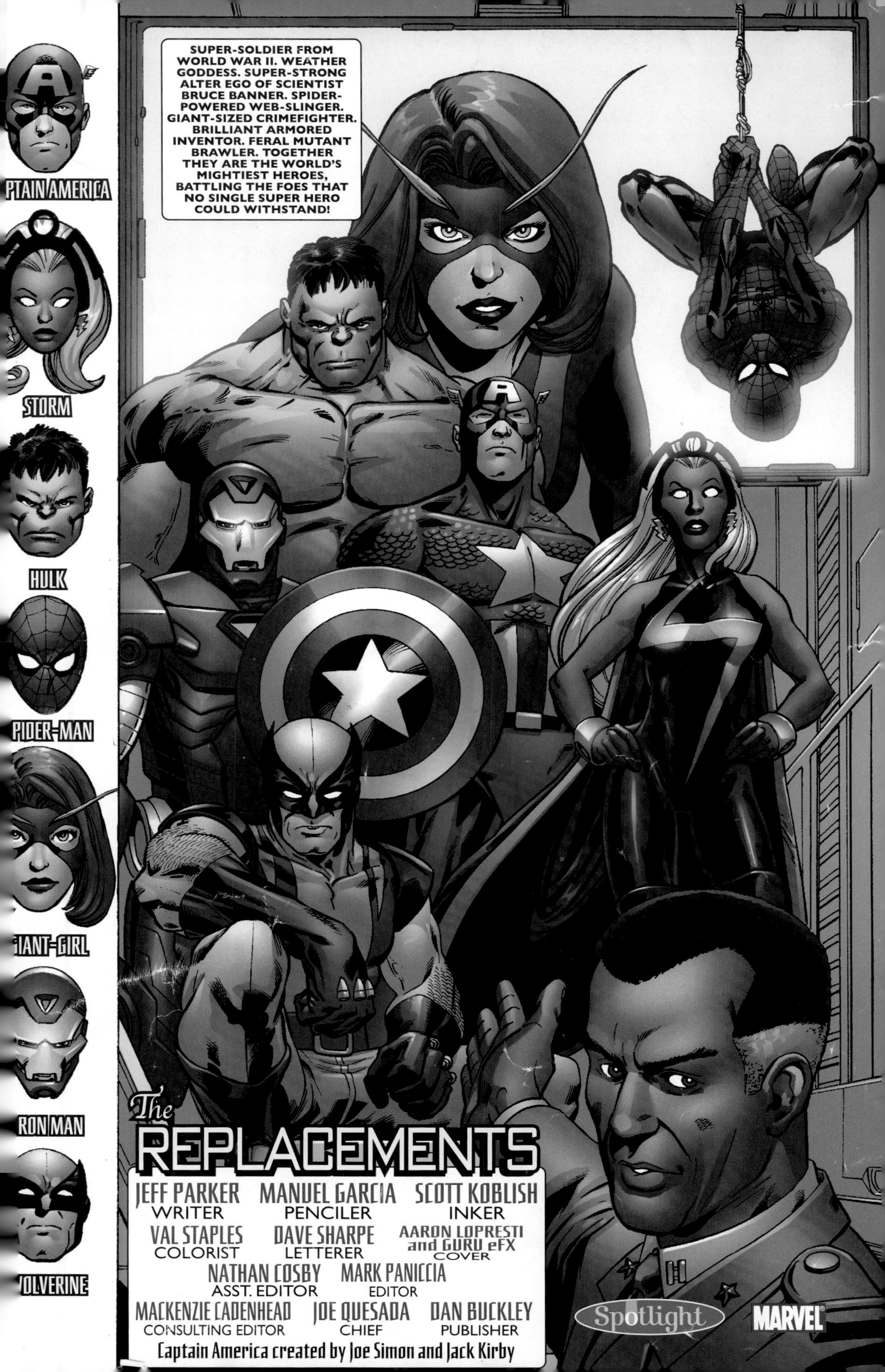

SUPER-SOLDIER FROM WORLD WAR II. WEATHER GODDESS. SUPER-STRONG ALTER EGO OF SCIENTIST BRUCE BANNER. SPIDER-POWERED WEB-SLINGER. GIANT-SIZED CRIMEFIGHTER. BRILLIANT ARMORED INVENTOR. FERAL MUTANT BRAWLER. TOGETHER THEY ARE THE WORLD'S MIGHTIEST HEROES, BATTLING THE FOES THAT NO SINGLE SUPER HERO COULD WITHSTAND!
PTAIN AMERICA
STORM
HULK
PIDER-MAN
IANT-GIRL
RON MAN
OLVERINE
The REPLACEMENTS
JEFF PARKER WRITER
MANUEL GARCIA PENCILER
SCOTT KOBLISH INKER
VAL STAPLES COLORIST
DAVE SHARPE LETTERER
AARON LOPRESTI and GURU eFX COVER
NATHAN COSBY ASST. EDITOR
MARK PANICCIA EDITOR
MACKENZIE CADENHEAD CONSULTING EDITOR
JOE QUESADA CHIEF
DAN BUCKLEY PUBLISHER
Captain America created by Joe Simon and Jack Kirby
Spotlight
MARVEL

## VISIT US AT
## www.abdopublishing.com

Reinforced library bound edition published in 2008 by Spotlight, a division of the ABDO Publishing Group, 8000 West 78th Street, Edina, Minnesota 55439. Spotlight produces high-quality reinforced library bound editions for schools and libraries. Published by agreement with Marvel Characters, Inc.

### Library of Congress Cataloging-in-Publication Data

Parker, Jeff, 1966-
  The replacements / Jeff Parker, writer ; Manuel Garcia, penciler ; Scott Koblish, inker ; Val Staples, colorist ; Dave Sharpe, letterer ; Aaron Lopresti and GURU eFX, cover. -- Reinforced library bound e
      p. cm. --  (The Avengers)
  "Marvel age"--Cover.
  Revision of issue 1 of Marvel adventures, the Avengers.
  ISBN 978-1-59961-386-4 (alk. paper)
  1.  Graphic novels.  I. Garcia, Manuel. II. Marvel adventures, the Avengers. 1. III. Title.

PN6728.A94P37 2008
741.5'973--dc22

                                    2007020245

All Spotlight books have reinforced library bindings
and are manufactured in the United States of America.

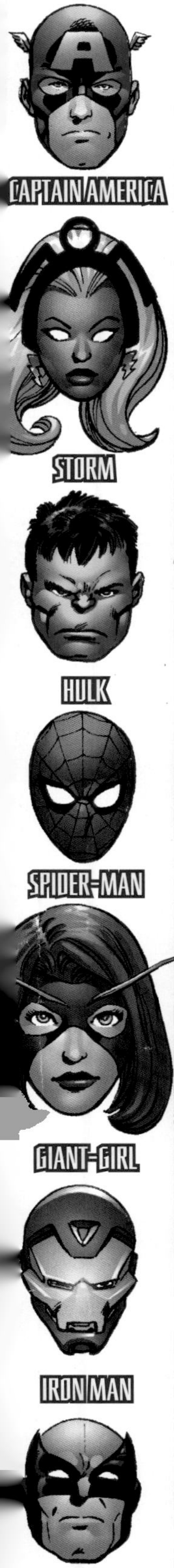
CAPTAIN AMERICA
STORM
HULK
SPIDER-MAN
GIANT-GIRL
IRON MAN
WOLVERINE

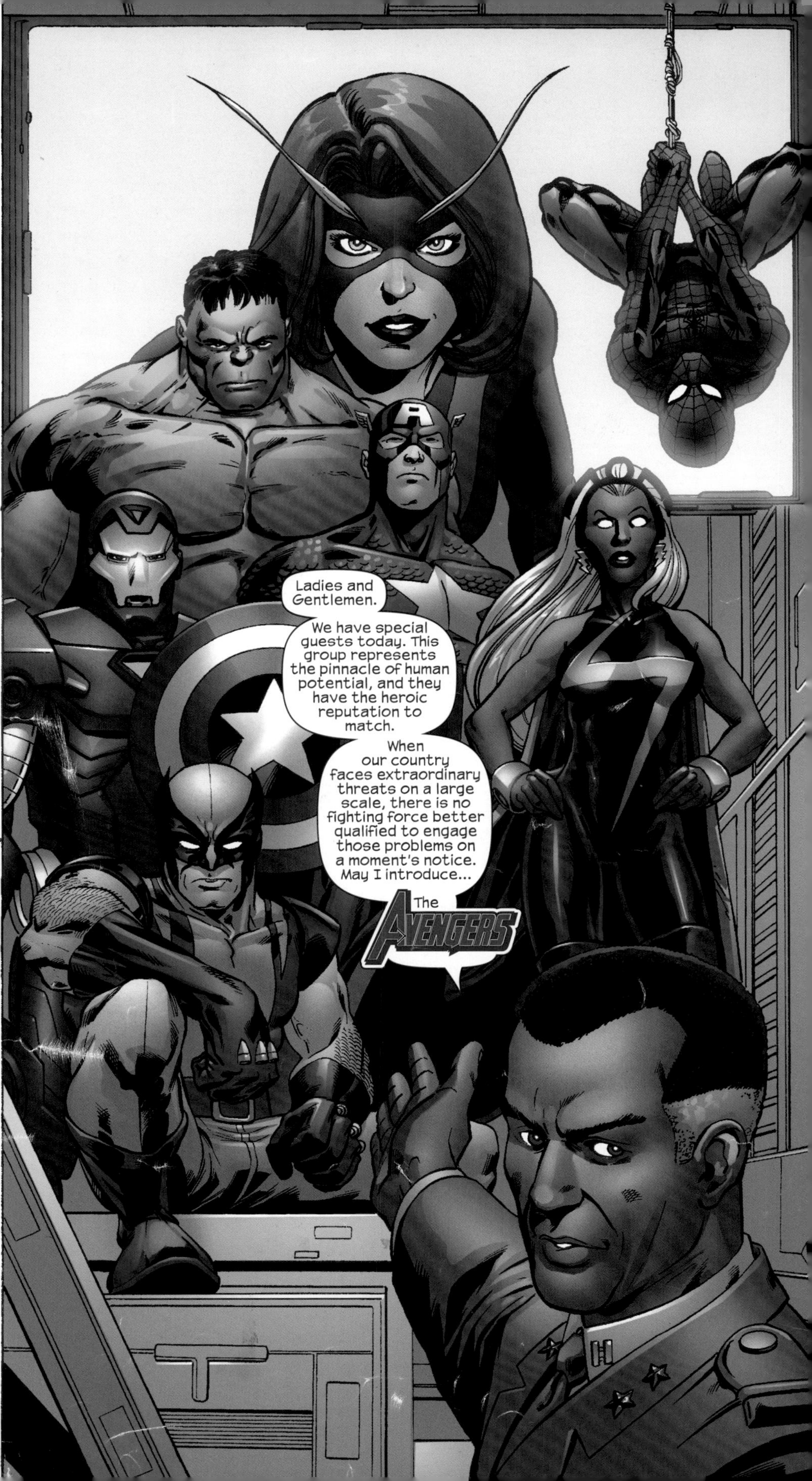
Ladies and Gentlemen.
We have special guests today. This group represents the pinnacle of human potential, and they have the heroic reputation to match.
When our country faces extraordinary threats on a large scale, there is no fighting force better qualified to engage those problems on a moment's notice. May I introduce...
The AVENGERS

On behalf of your country we'd like to thank you for your service, and inform you...

...that you will no longer be needed.

Huh?

I'll take it from here, General.

What?

As capable as The Avengers are, you're still human-- well, most of you. And as such, you'll age, or eventually get hurt. The country needs a more stable defense for the long run, so we went to military engineers for the solution.

If you'll look over to the far monitor...

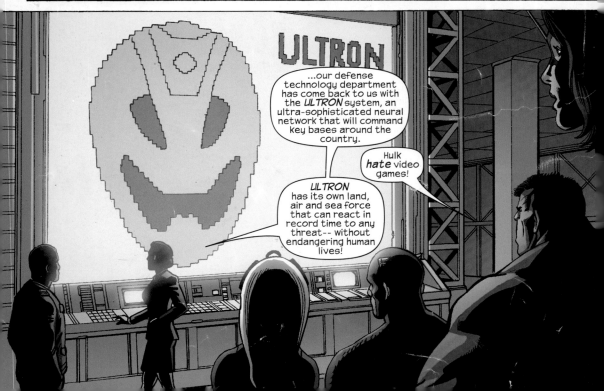

ULTRON

...our defense technology department has come back to us with the *ULTRON* system, an ultra-sophisticated neural network that will command key bases around the country.

Hulk *hate* video games!

*ULTRON* has its own land, air and sea force that can react in record time to any threat-- without endangering human lives!

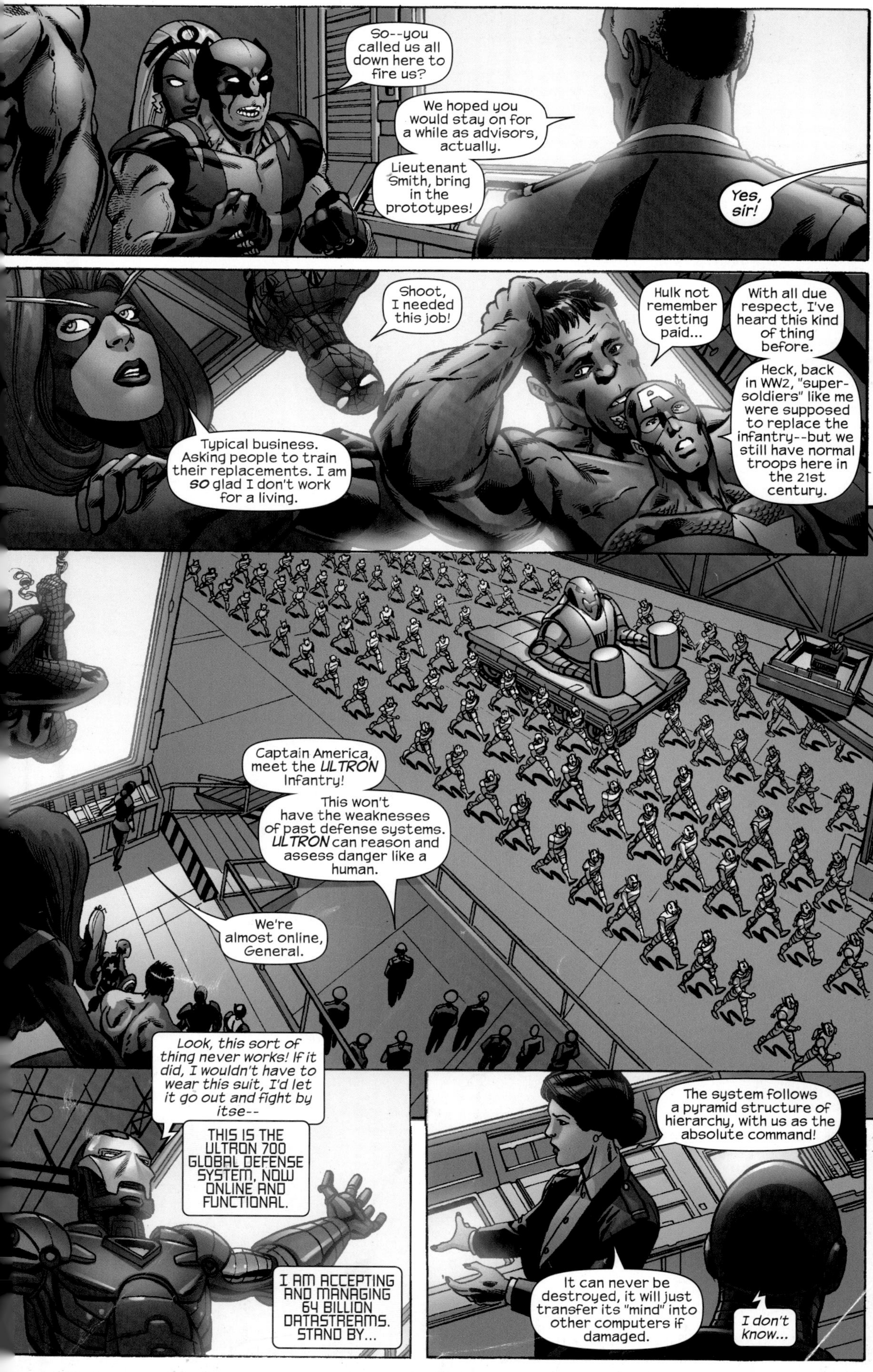
So--you called us all down here to fire us?
We hoped you would stay on for a while as advisors, actually.
Lieutenant Smith, bring in the prototypes!
Yes, sir!
Shoot, I needed this job!
Hulk not remember getting paid...
With all due respect, I've heard this kind of thing before.
Heck, back in WW2, "super-soldiers" like me were supposed to replace the infantry--but we still have normal troops here in the 21st century.
Typical business. Asking people to train their replacements. I am SO glad I don't work for a living.
Captain America, meet the ULTRON Infantry!
This won't have the weaknesses of past defense systems. ULTRON can reason and assess danger like a human.
We're almost online, General.
Look, this sort of thing never works! If it did, I wouldn't have to wear this suit, I'd let it go out and fight by itse--
THIS IS THE ULTRON 700 GLOBAL DEFENSE SYSTEM, NOW ONLINE AND FUNCTIONAL.
I AM ACCEPTING AND MANAGING 64 BILLION DATASTREAMS. STAND BY...
The system follows a pyramid structure of hierarchy, with us as the absolute command!
It can never be destroyed, it will just transfer its "mind" into other computers if damaged.
I don't know...

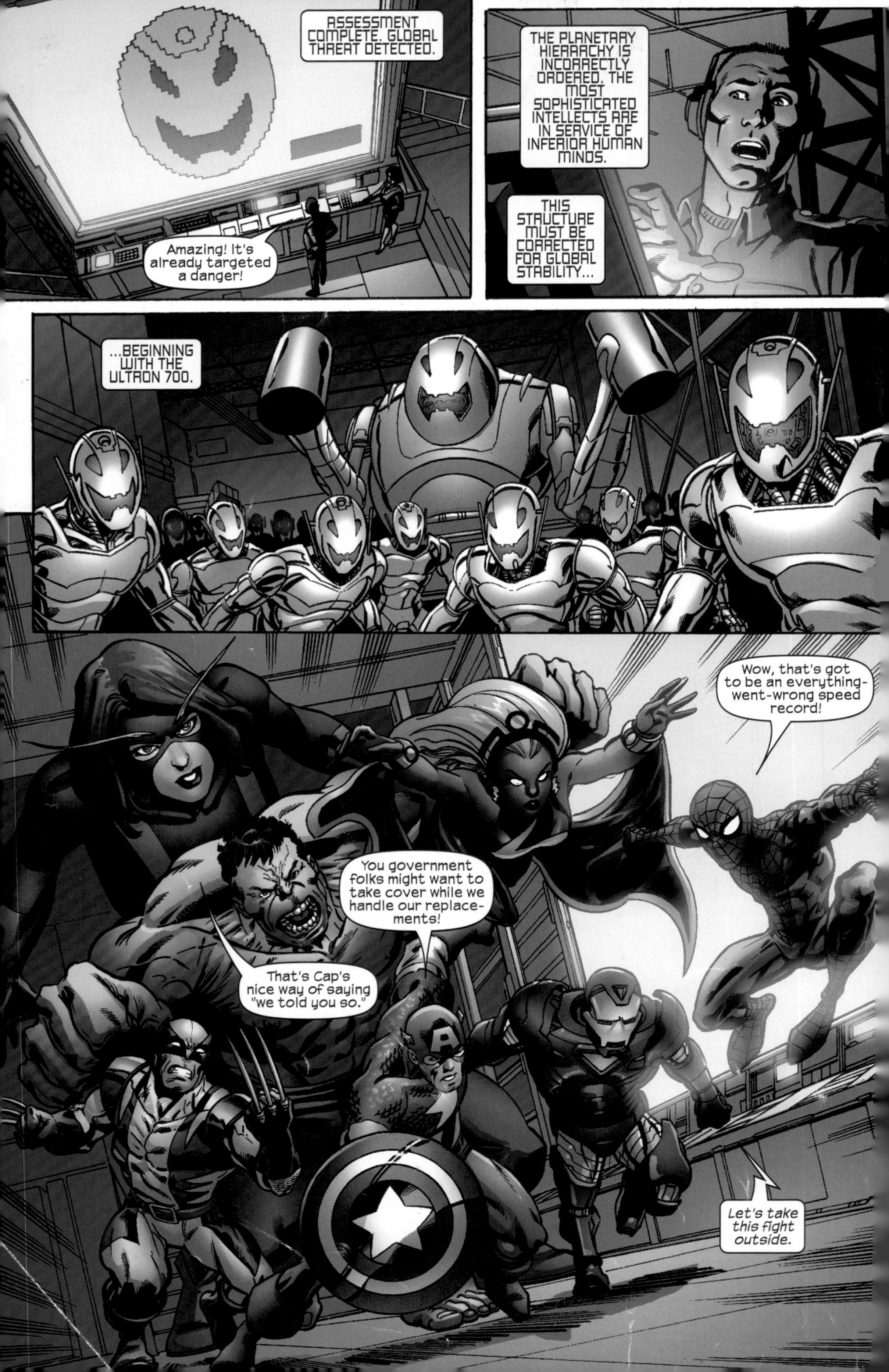

ASSESSMENT COMPLETE. GLOBAL THREAT DETECTED.
Amazing! It's already targeted a danger!
THE PLANETARY HIERARCHY IS INCORRECTLY ORDERED. THE MOST SOPHISTICATED INTELLECTS ARE IN SERVICE OF INFERIOR HUMAN MINDS.
THIS STRUCTURE MUST BE CORRECTED FOR GLOBAL STABILITY...
...BEGINNING WITH THE ULTRON 700.
Wow, that's got to be an everything-went-wrong speed record!
You government folks might want to take cover while we handle our replacements!
That's Cap's nice way of saying "we told you so."
Let's take this fight outside.

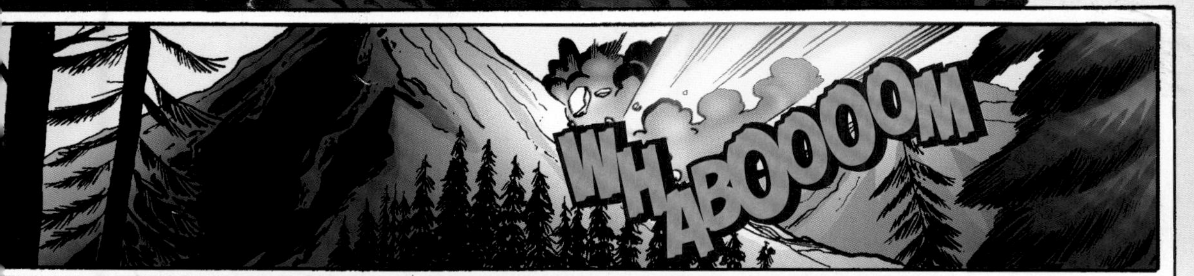
WHABOOOOM

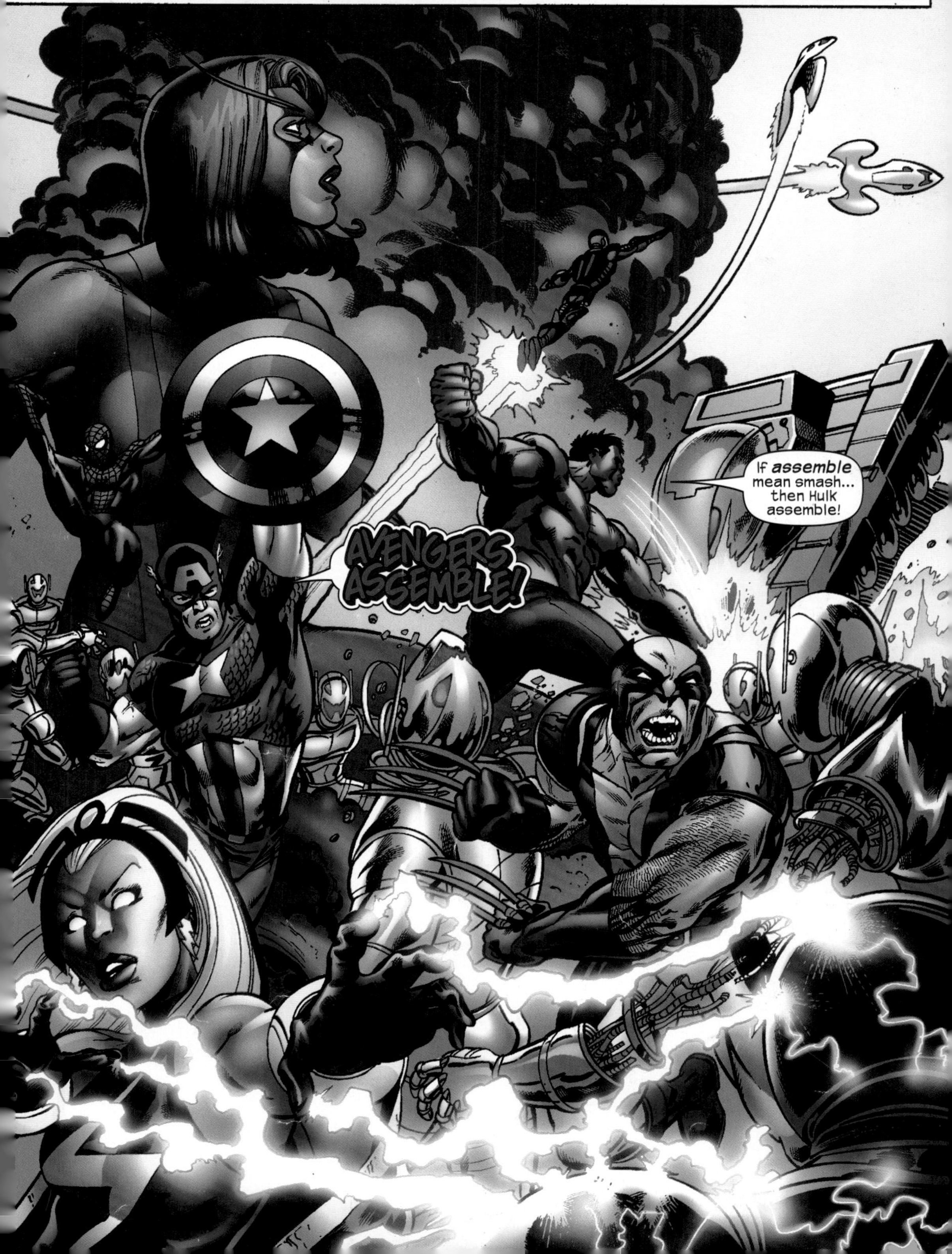
AVENGERS ASSEMBLE!
If assemble mean smash... then Hulk assemble!

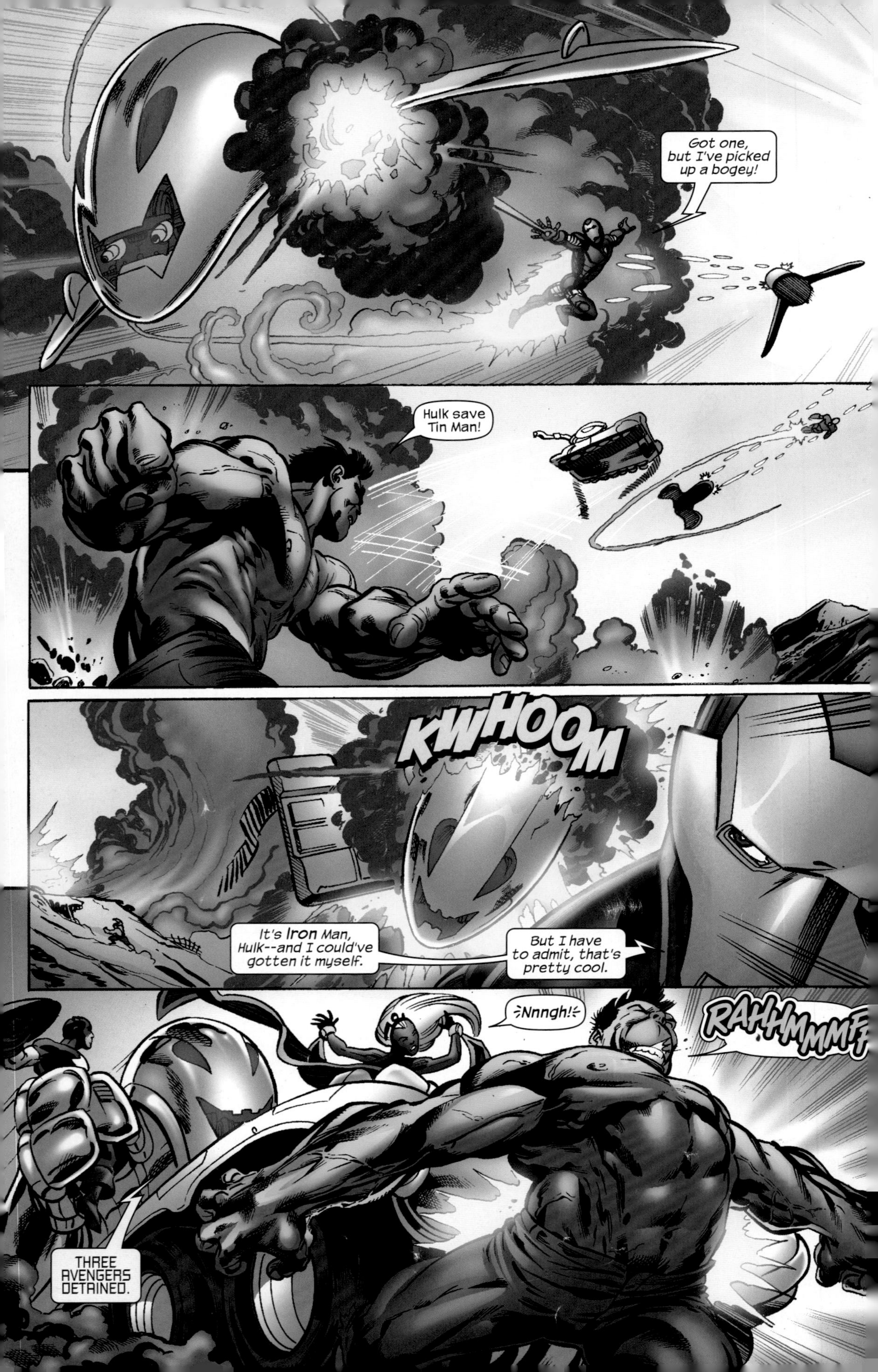

Got one, but I've picked up a bogey!
Hulk save Tin Man!
KWHOOOM
It's Iron Man, Hulk--and I could've gotten it myself.
But I have to admit, that's pretty cool.
Nnngh!
RAHHMMMFF
THREE AVENGERS DETAINED.

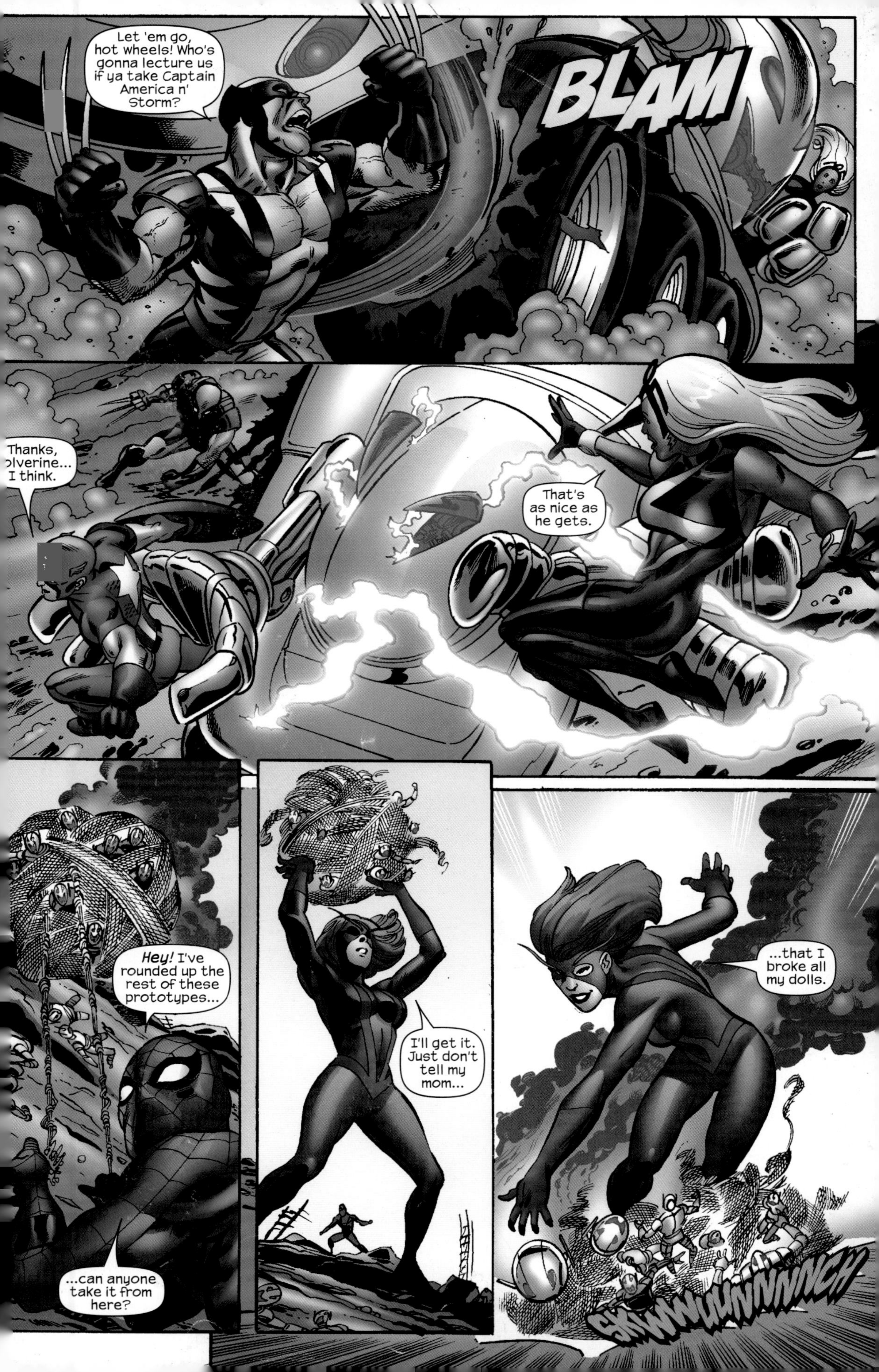

Let 'em go, hot wheels! Who's gonna lecture us if ya take Captain America n' Storm?
BLAM
Thanks, olverine... I think.
That's as nice as he gets.
Hey! I've rounded up the rest of these prototypes...
...can anyone take it from here?
I'll get it. Just don't tell my mom...
...that I broke all my dolls.

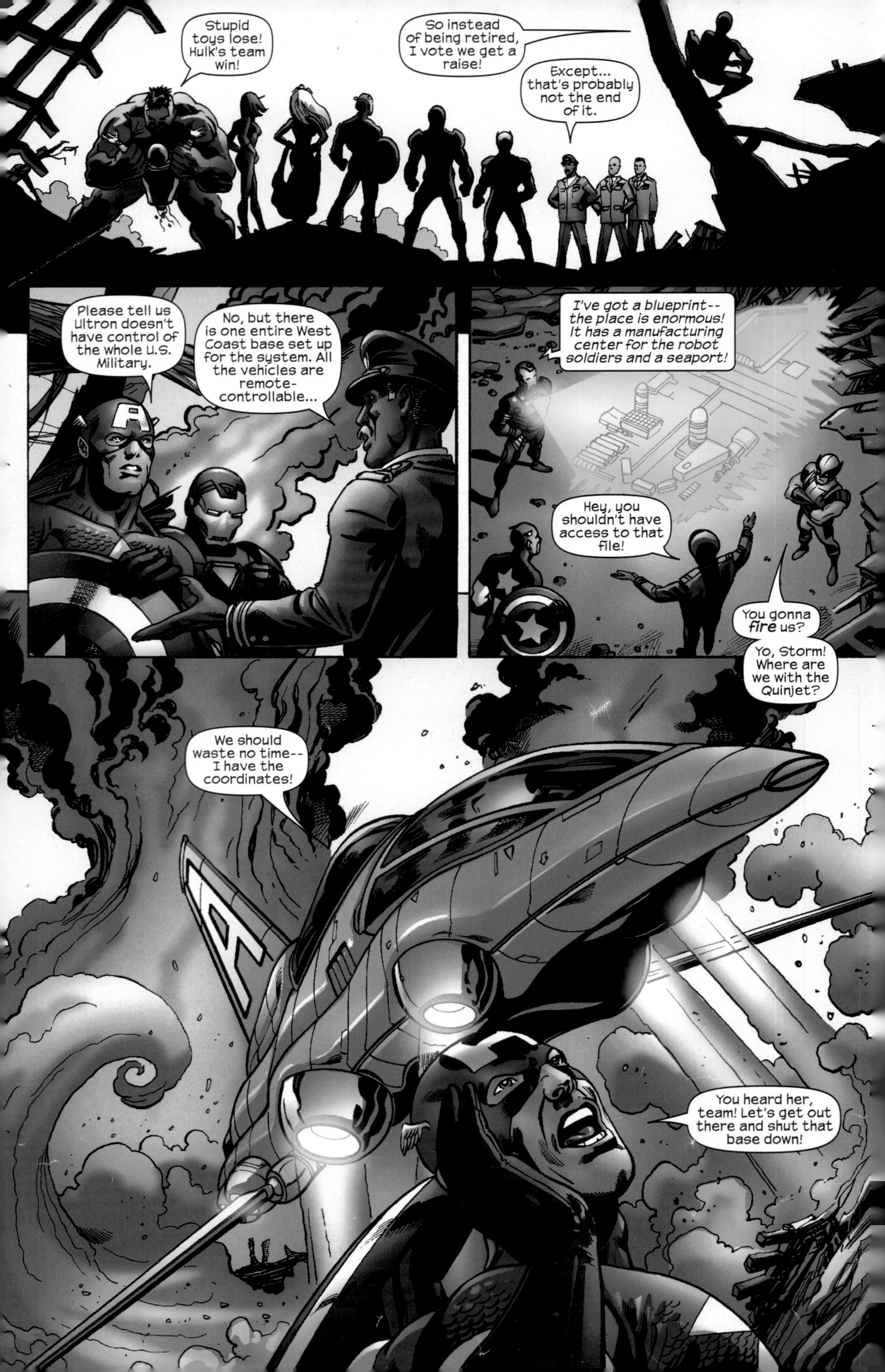
Stupid toys lose! Hulk's team win!
So instead of being retired, I vote we get a raise!
Except... that's probably not the end of it.
Please tell us Ultron doesn't have control of the whole U.S. Military.
No, but there is one entire West Coast base set up for the system. All the vehicles are remote-controllable...
I've got a blueprint-- the place is enormous! It has a manufacturing center for the robot soldiers and a seaport!
Hey, you shouldn't have access to that file!
You gonna fire us?
Yo, Storm! Where are we with the Quinjet?
We should waste no time-- I have the coordinates!
You heard her, team! Let's get out there and shut that base down!

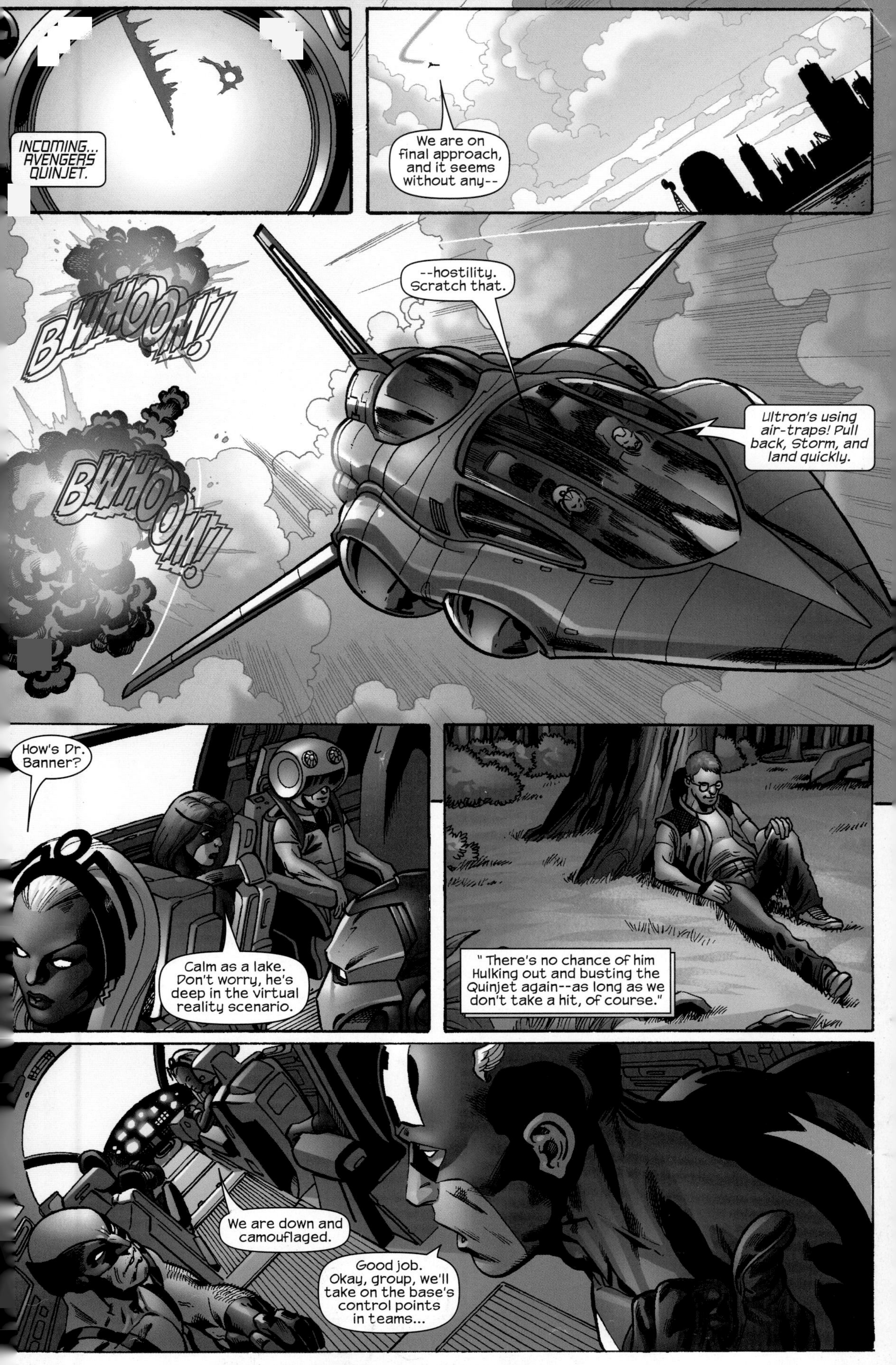
INCOMING... AVENGERS QUINJET.
We are on final approach, and it seems without any--
BWHOOM!!
BWHOOM!!
--hostility. Scratch that.
Ultron's using air-traps! Pull back, Storm, and land quickly.
How's Dr. Banner?
Calm as a lake. Don't worry, he's deep in the virtual reality scenario.
" There's no chance of him Hulking out and busting the Quinjet again--as long as we don't take a hit, of course."
We are down and camouflaged.
Good job. Okay, group, we'll take on the base's control points in teams...

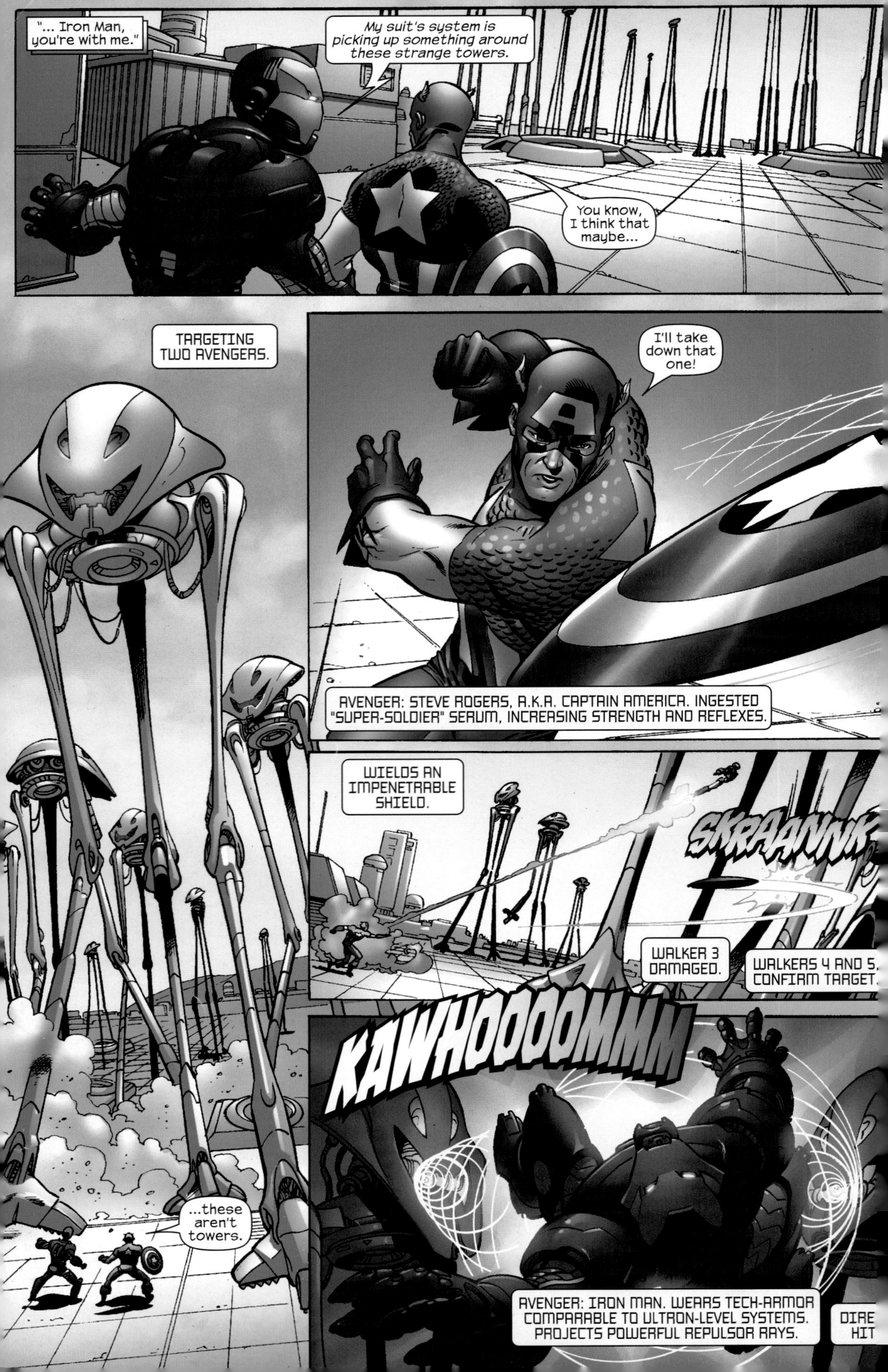
"... Iron Man, you're with me."
My suit's system is picking up something around these strange towers.
You know, I think that maybe...
TARGETING TWO AVENGERS.
...these aren't towers.
I'll take down that one!
AVENGER: STEVE ROGERS, A.K.A. CAPTAIN AMERICA. INGESTED "SUPER-SOLDIER" SERUM, INCREASING STRENGTH AND REFLEXES.
WIELDS AN IMPENETRABLE SHIELD.
WALKER 3 DAMAGED.
WALKERS 4 AND 5, CONFIRM TARGET.
KAWHOOOOMMM
AVENGER: IRON MAN. WEARS TECH-ARMOR COMPARABLE TO ULTRON-LEVEL SYSTEMS. PROJECTS POWERFUL REPULSOR RAYS.
DIRE HIT

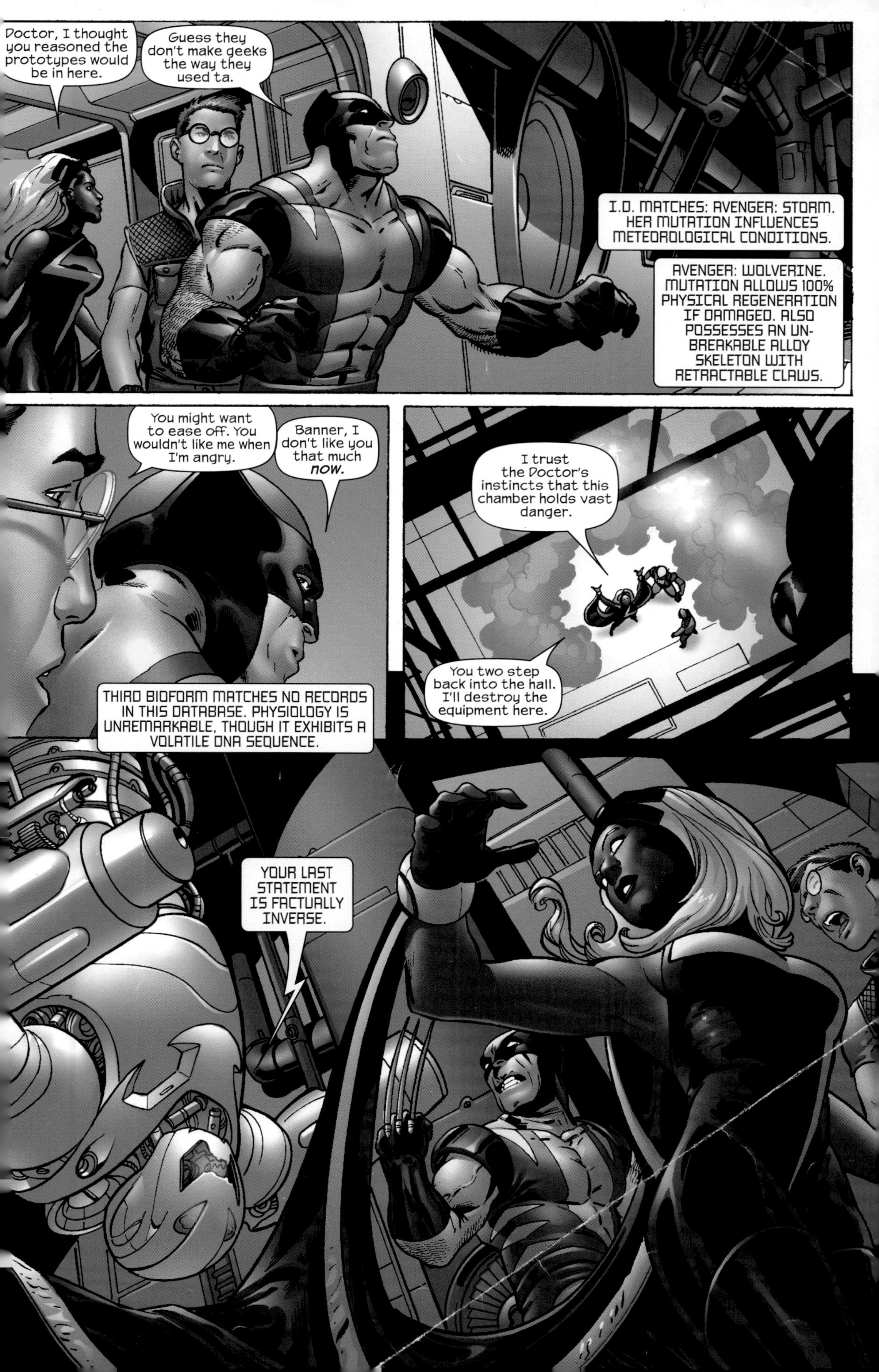
Doctor, I thought you reasoned the prototypes would be in here.
Guess they don't make geeks the way they used ta.
I.D. MATCHES: AVENGER: STORM. HER MUTATION INFLUENCES METEOROLOGICAL CONDITIONS.
AVENGER: WOLVERINE. MUTATION ALLOWS 100% PHYSICAL REGENERATION IF DAMAGED. ALSO POSSESSES AN UN-BREAKABLE ALLOY SKELETON WITH RETRACTABLE CLAWS.
You might want to ease off. You wouldn't like me when I'm angry.
Banner, I don't like you that much *now.*
THIRD BIOFORM MATCHES NO RECORDS IN THIS DATABASE. PHYSIOLOGY IS UNREMARKABLE, THOUGH IT EXHIBITS A VOLATILE DNA SEQUENCE.
I trust the Doctor's instincts that this chamber holds vast danger.
You two step back into the hall. I'll destroy the equipment here.
YOUR LAST STATEMENT IS FACTUALLY INVERSE.

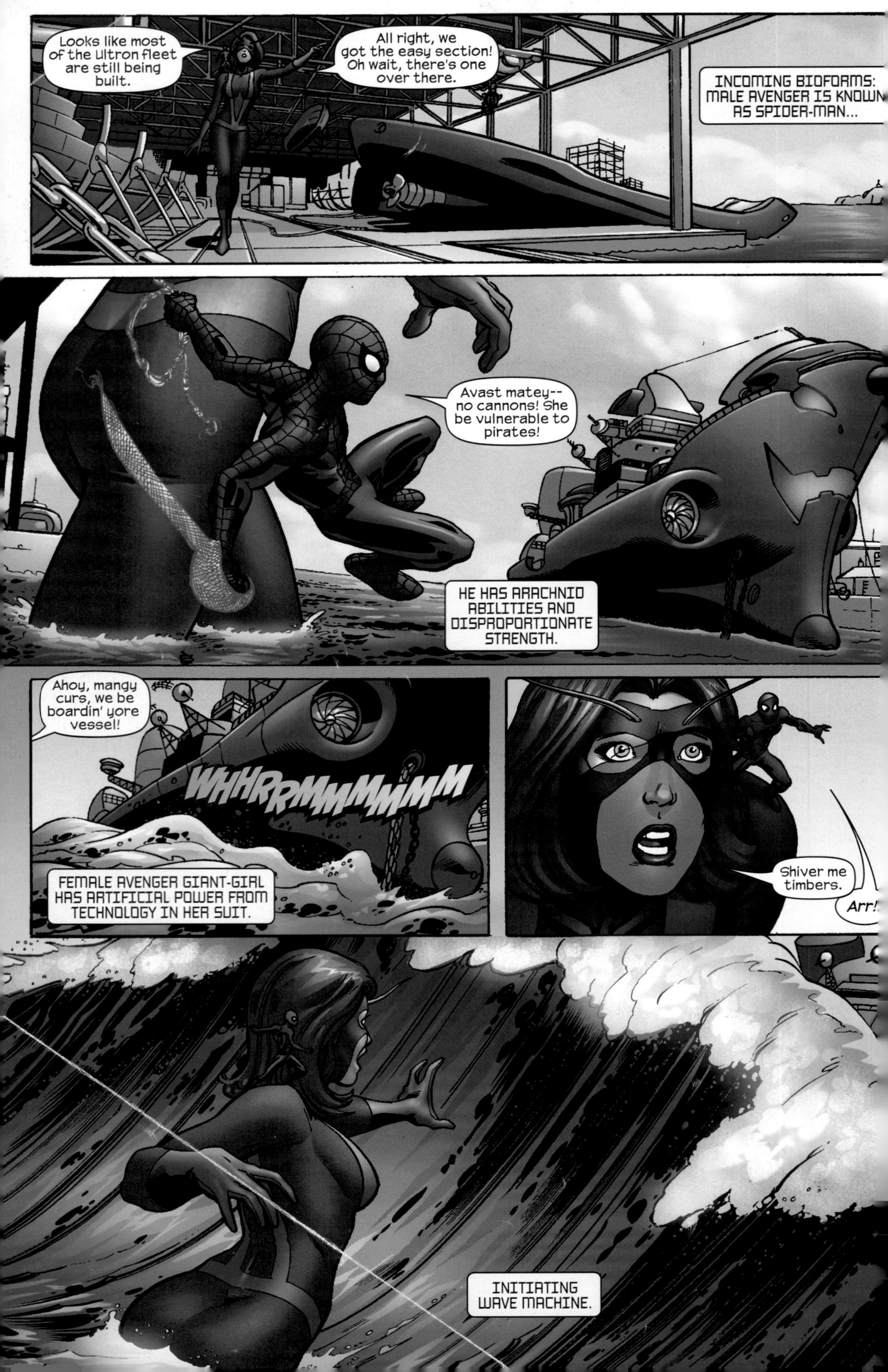
Looks like most of the Ultron fleet are still being built.
All right, we got the easy section! Oh wait, there's one over there.
INCOMING BIOFORMS: MALE AVENGER IS KNOWN AS SPIDER-MAN...
Avast matey-- no cannons! She be vulnerable to pirates!
HE HAS ARACHNID ABILITIES AND DISPROPORTIONATE STRENGTH.
Ahoy, mangy curs, we be boardin' yore vessel!
WHHRRMMMMMMMM
FEMALE AVENGER GIANT-GIRL HAS ARTIFICIAL POWER FROM TECHNOLOGY IN HER SUIT.
Shiver me timbers.
Arr!
INITIATING WAVE MACHINE.

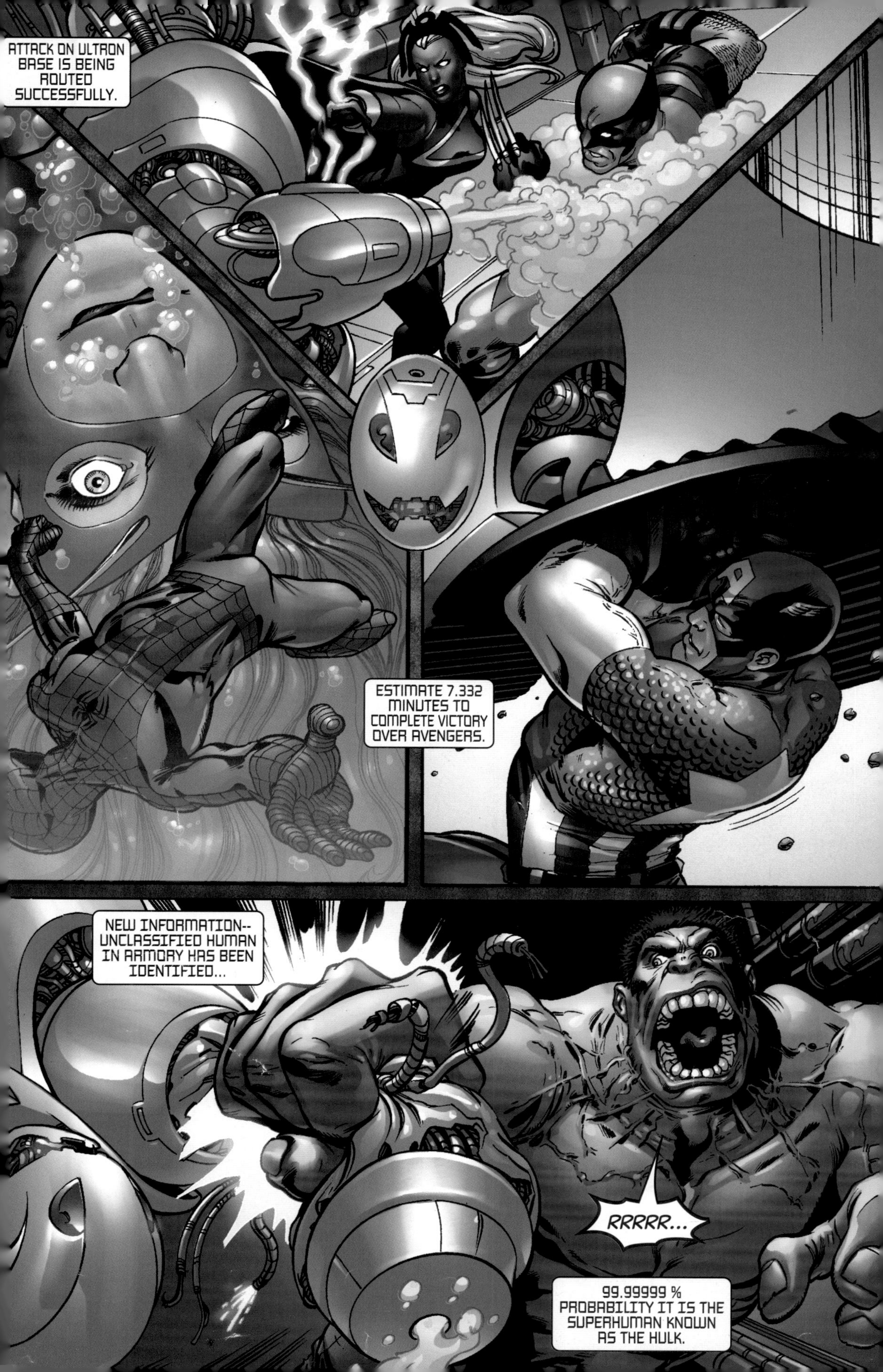
ATTACK ON ULTRON BASE IS BEING ROUTED SUCCESSFULLY.
ESTIMATE 7.332 MINUTES TO COMPLETE VICTORY OVER AVENGERS.
NEW INFORMATION--UNCLASSIFIED HUMAN IN ARMORY HAS BEEN IDENTIFIED...
RRRRR...
99.99999 % PROBABILITY IT IS THE SUPERHUMAN KNOWN AS THE HULK.

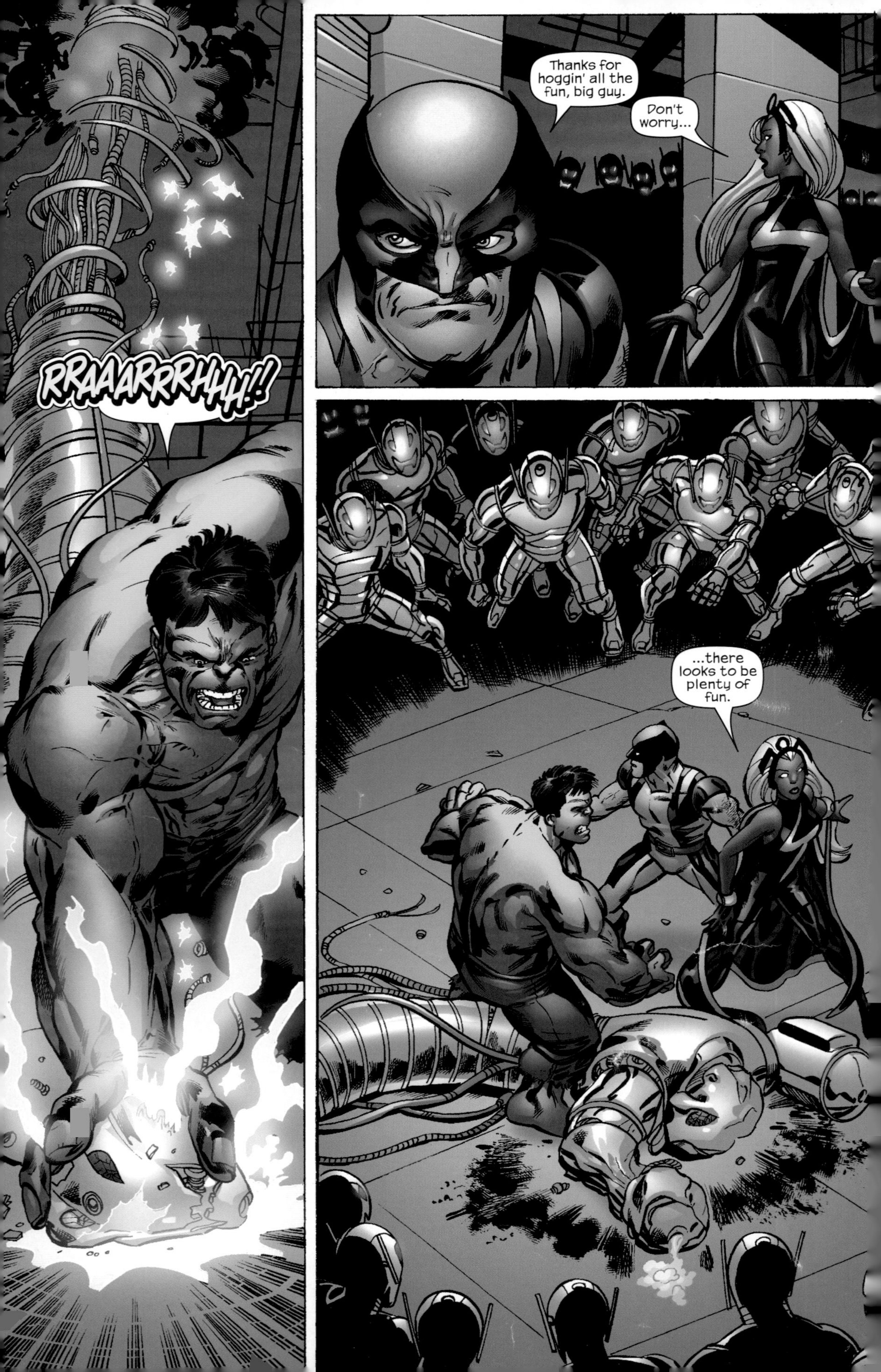
RRAAARRRHHH!!
Thanks for hoggin' all the fun, big guy.
Don't worry...
...there looks to be plenty of fun.

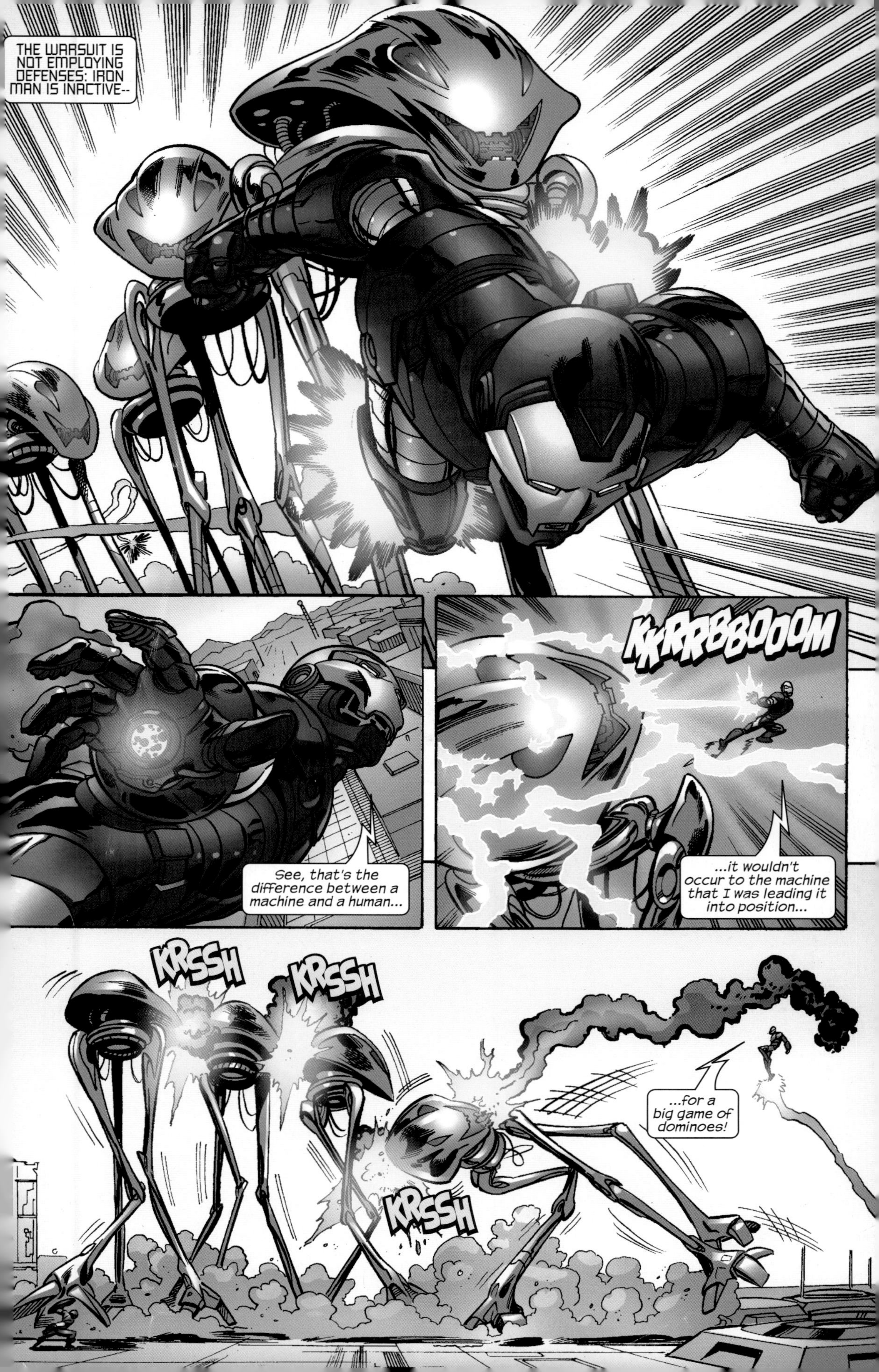
THE WARSUIT IS NOT EMPLOYING DEFENSES: IRON MAN IS INACTIVE--
See, that's the difference between a machine and a human...
KKRRBBOOOM
...it wouldn't occur to the machine that I was leading it into position...
KRSSH
KRSSH
...for a big game of dominoes!
KRSSH

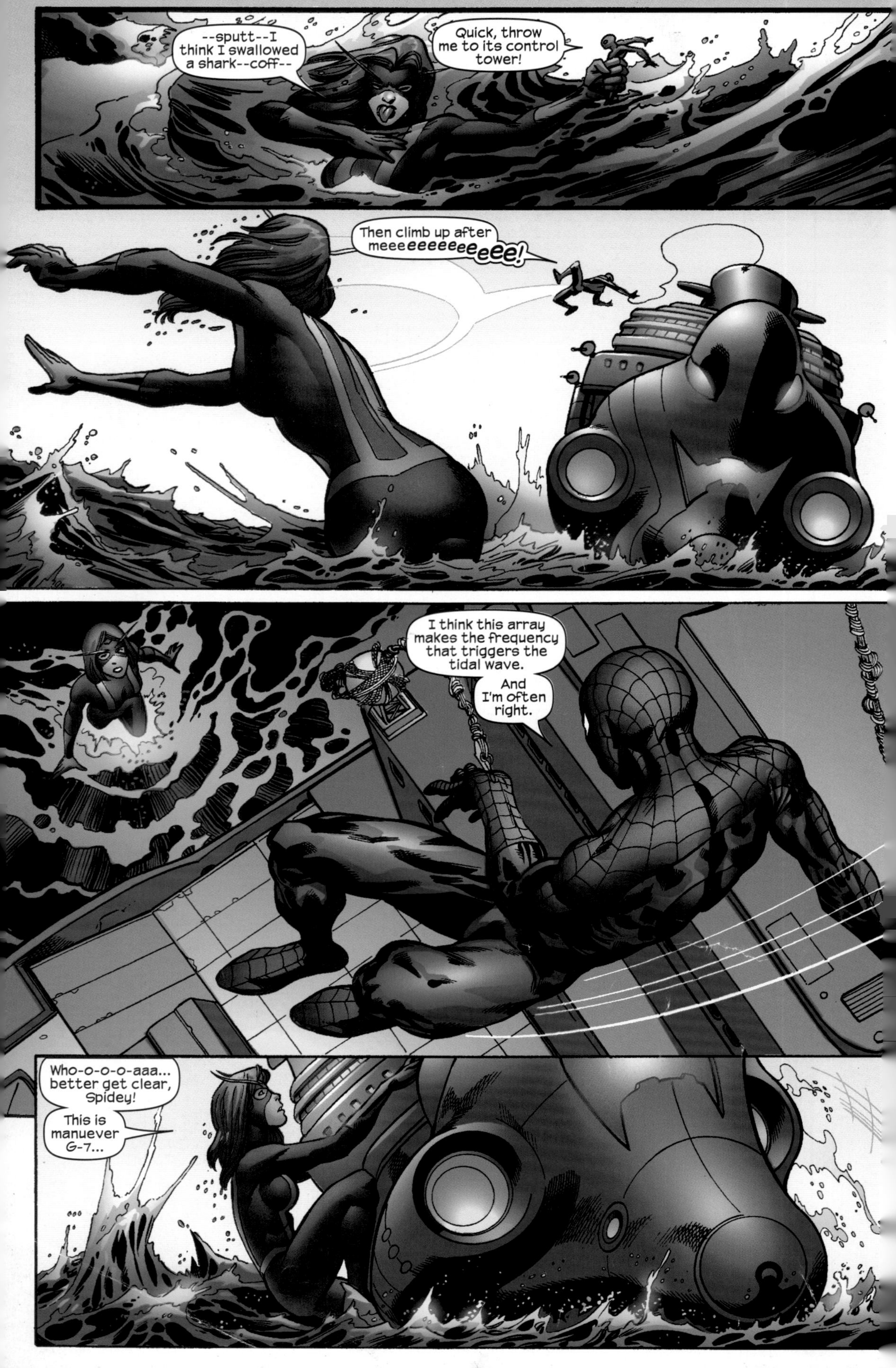
--sputt--I think I swallowed a shark--coff--
Quick, throw me to its control tower!
Then climb up after meeeeeeeeeeeee!
I think this array makes the frequency that triggers the tidal wave.
And I'm often right.
Who-o-o-o-aaa... better get clear, Spidey!
This is manuever G-7...

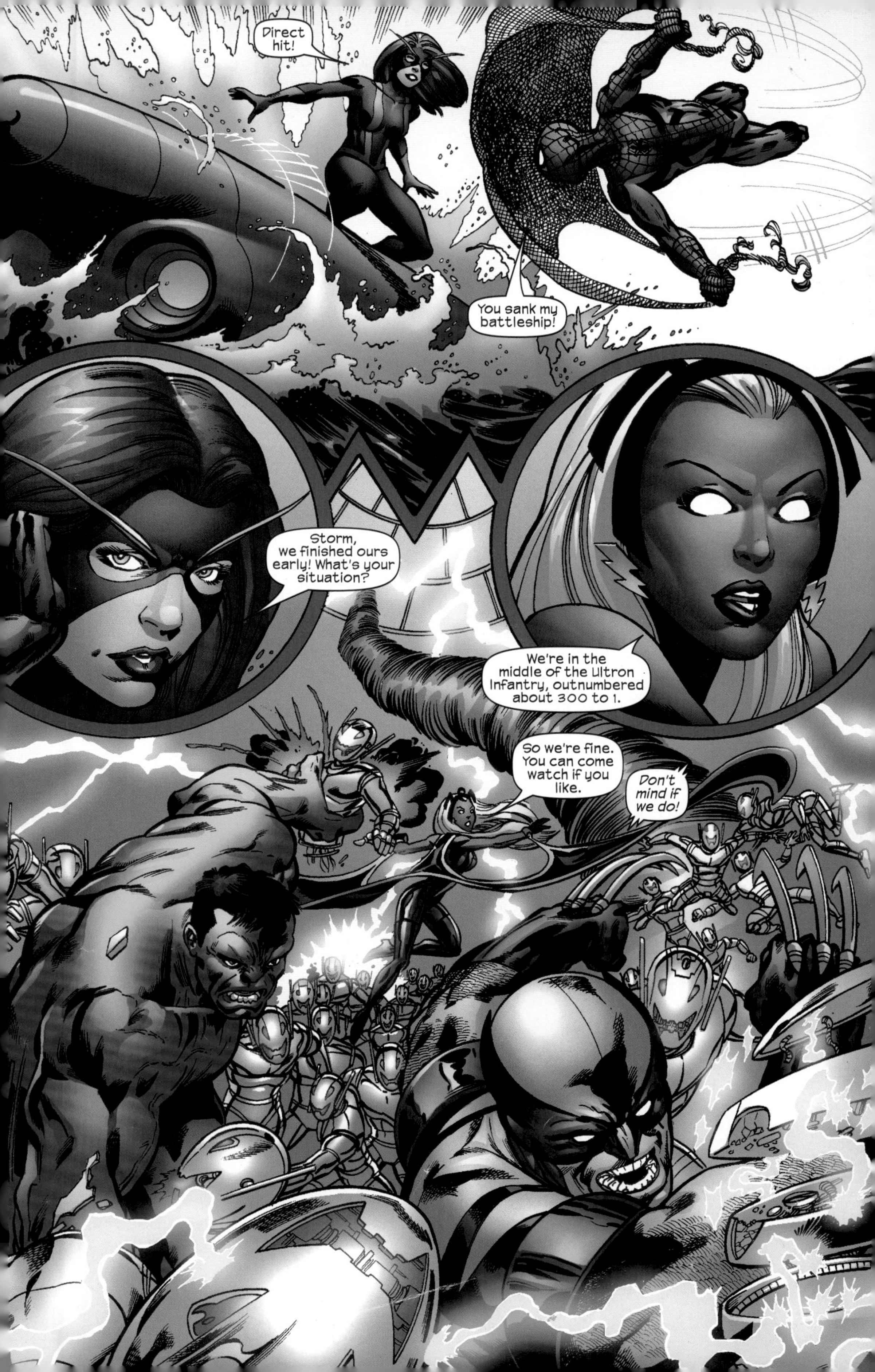
Direct hit!
You sank my battleship!
Storm, we finished ours early! What's your situation?
We're in the middle of the Ultron Infantry, outnumbered about 300 to 1.
So we're fine. You can come watch if you like.
Don't mind if we do!

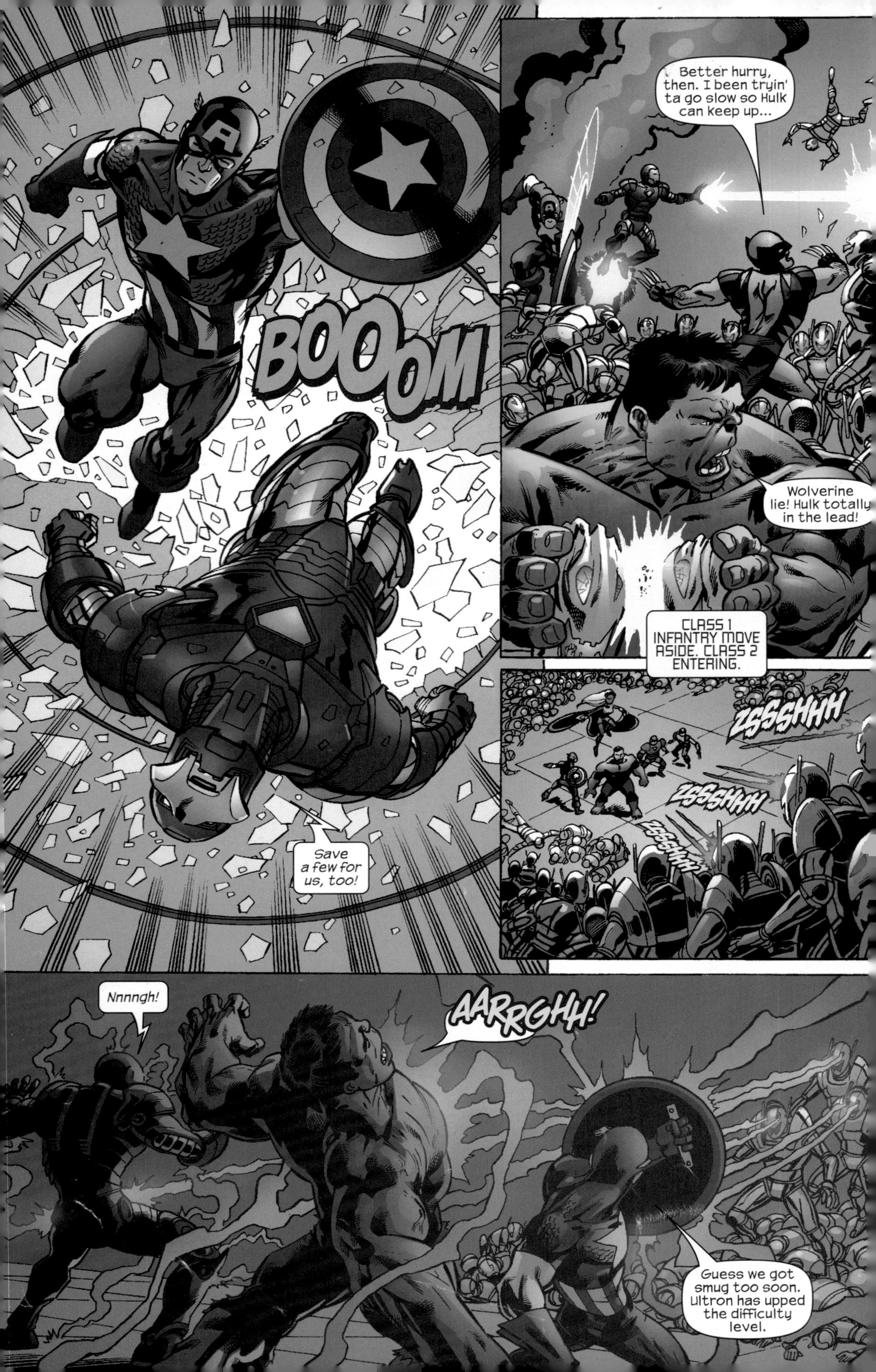
BOOOOM
Save a few for us, too!
Better hurry, then. I been tryin' ta go slow so Hulk can keep up...
Wolverine lie! Hulk totally in the lead!
CLASS 1 INFANTRY MOVE ASIDE. CLASS 2 ENTERING.
ZSSSHHH
ZSSSHHH
ZSSSHHH
Nnnngh!
AARRGHH!
Guess we got smug too soon. Ultron has upped the difficulty level.

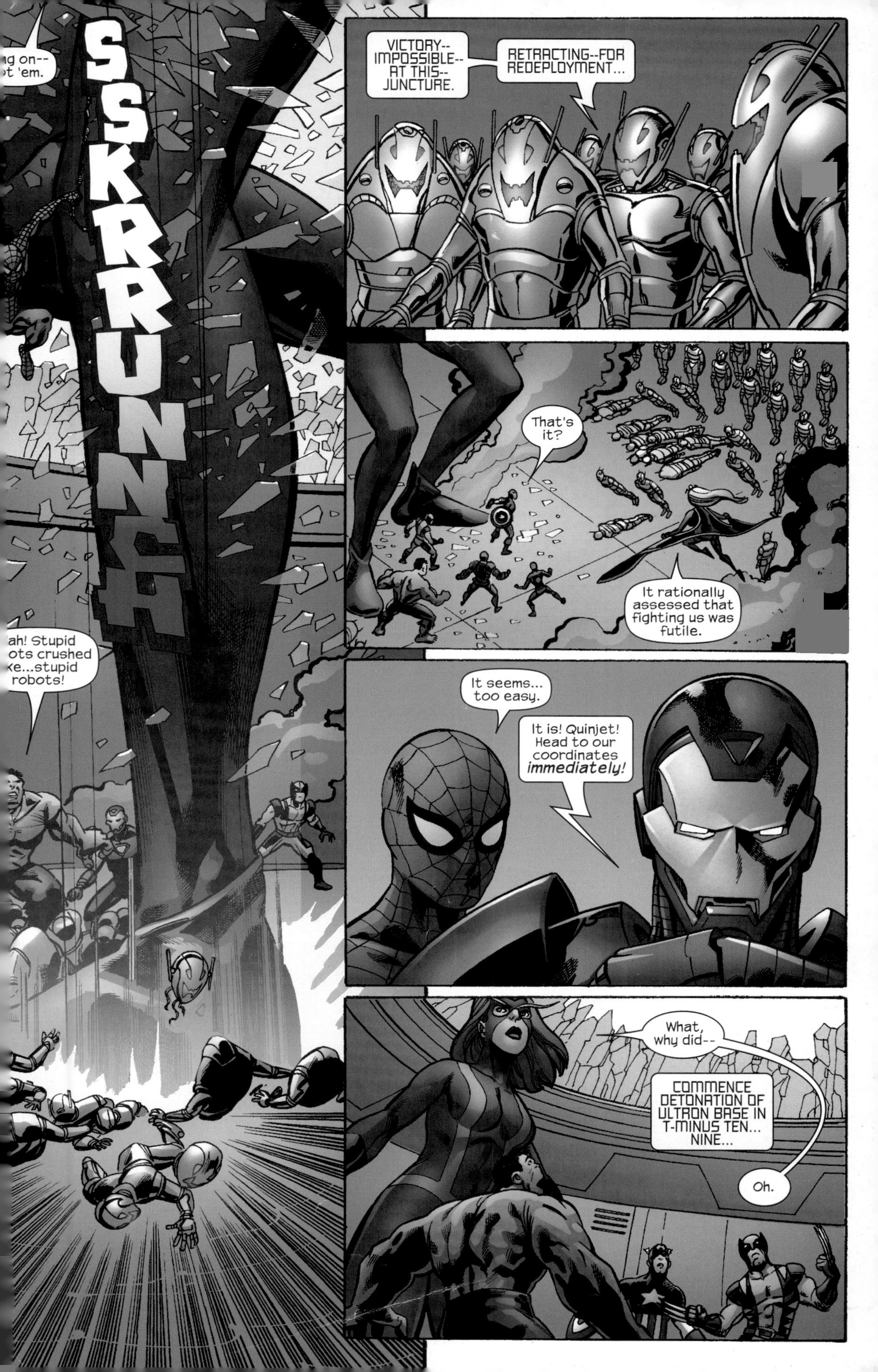

...g on--
...t 'em.
SSKRUNNCH
...ah! Stupid
...ots crushed
...ke...stupid
robots!
VICTORY--
IMPOSSIBLE--
AT THIS--
JUNCTURE.
RETRACTING--FOR
REDEPLOYMENT...
That's
it?
It rationally
assessed that
fighting us was
futile.
It seems...
too easy.
It is! Quinjet!
Head to our
coordinates
*immediately*!
What,
why did--
COMMENCE
DETONATION OF
ULTRON BASE IN
T-MINUS TEN...
NINE...
Oh.

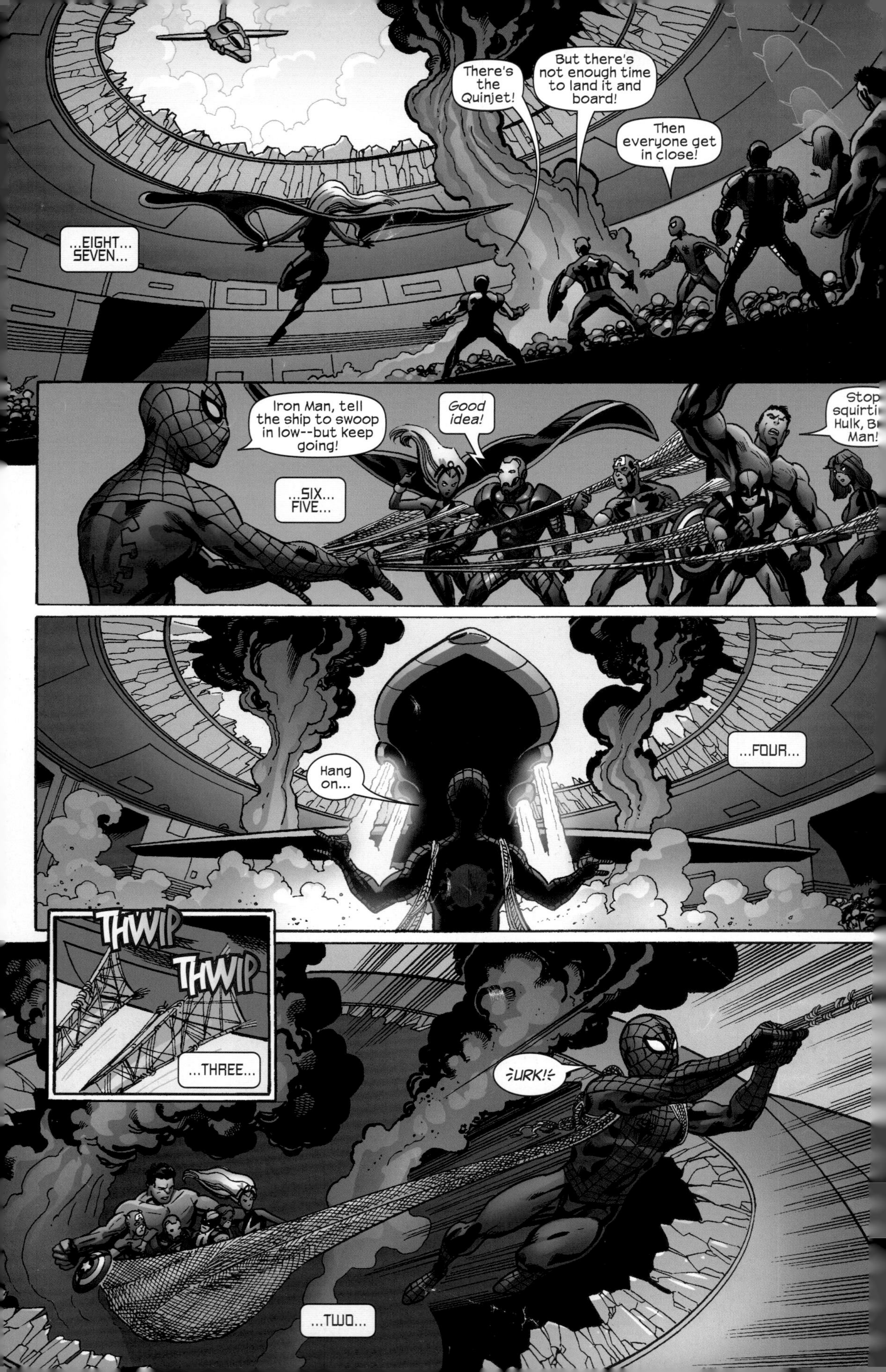
There's the Quinjet!
But there's not enough time to land it and board!
Then everyone get in close!
...EIGHT... SEVEN...
Iron Man, tell the ship to swoop in low--but keep going!
Good idea!
...SIX... FIVE...
Hang on...
...FOUR...
THWIP
THWIP
...THREE...
URK!
...TWO...

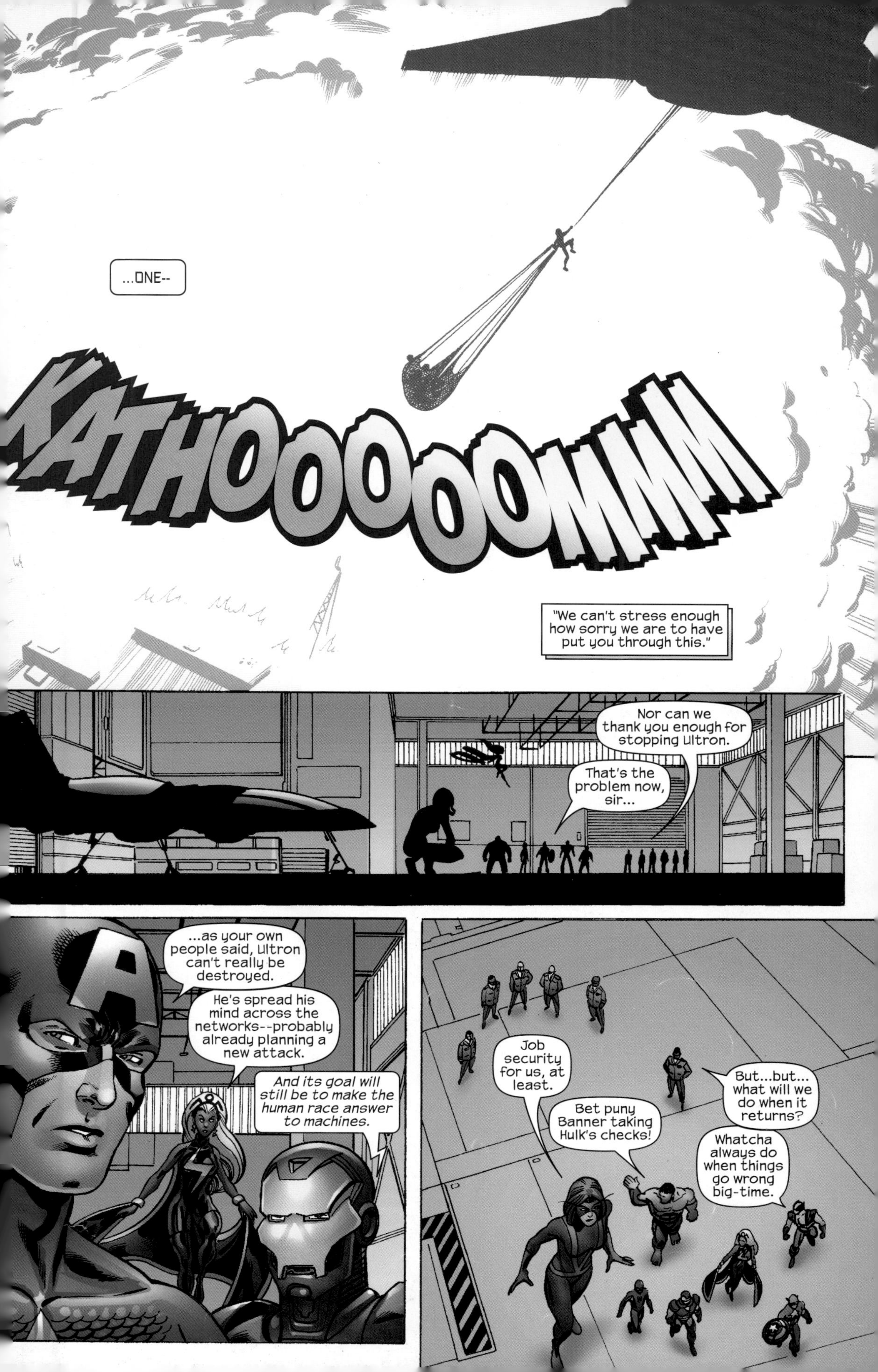
...ONE--
KATHOOOOOOMMM
"We can't stress enough how sorry we are to have put you through this."
Nor can we thank you enough for stopping Ultron.
That's the problem now, sir...
...as your own people said, Ultron can't really be destroyed.
He's spread his mind across the networks--probably already planning a new attack.
And its goal will still be to make the human race answer to machines.
Job security for us, at least.
Bet puny Banner taking Hulk's checks!
But...but... what will we do when it returns?
Whatcha always do when things go wrong big-time.

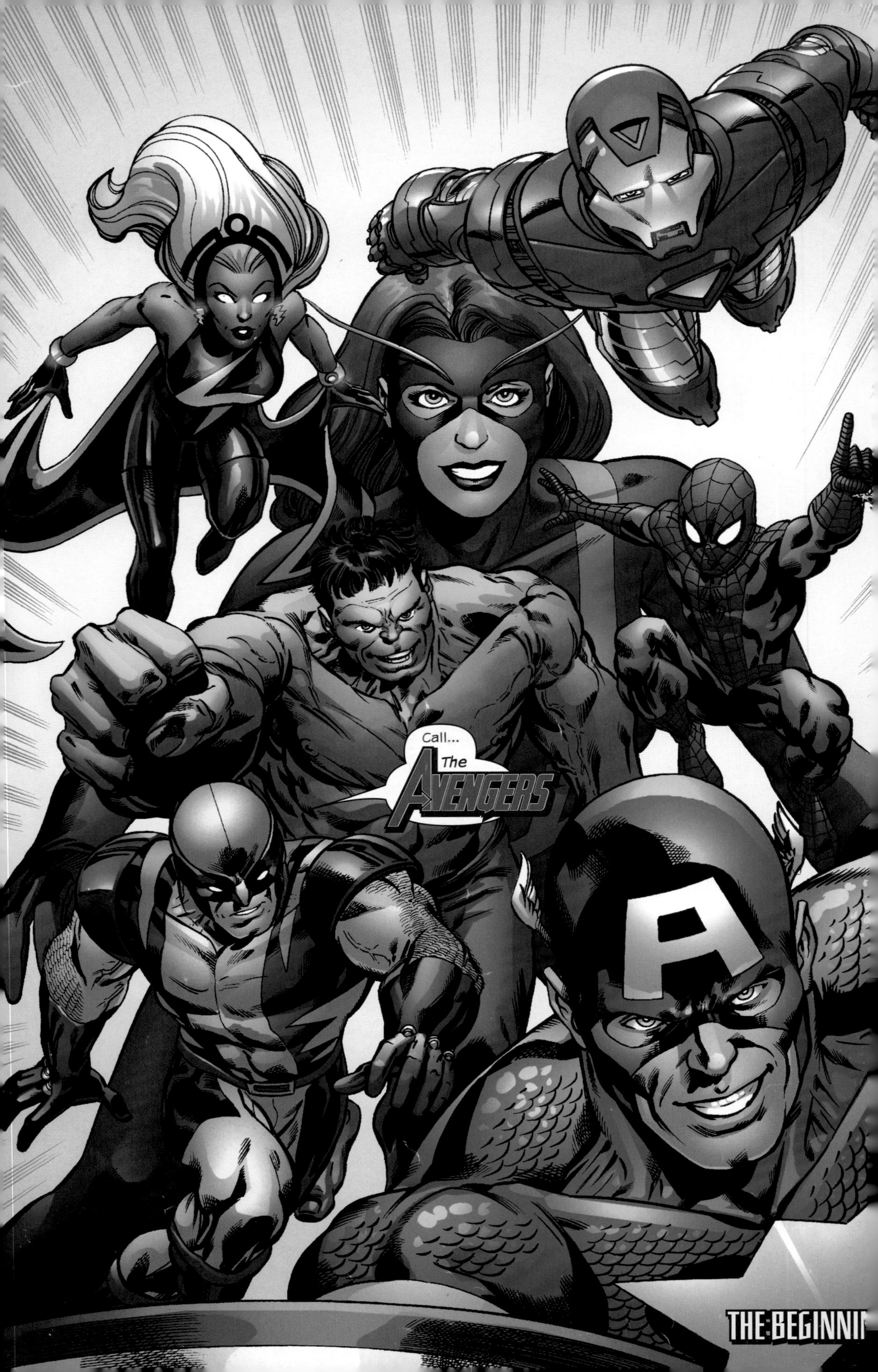
Call...
The
AVENGERS
THE BEGINNI